AN
ILLUSIONARY
TALE

OPT

BY
ARLINE AND
JOSEPH BAUM

PUFFIN BOOKS

For Helen Canfield
who believes that elephants do *live in barns*
For our friends in the CR at HPL
who encouraged and supported us
For Deborah, Barbara, and especially
Stephanie, who directed the show—helped put
it on the road—and whose undying enthusiasm
sustained us.

PUFFIN BOOKS
A Division of Penguin Books USA Inc.
375 Hudson Street, New York, New York 10014
Penguin Books Ltd, 27 Wrights Lane, London W8 5TZ, England
Penguin Books Australia Ltd, Ringwood, Victoria, Australia
Penguin Books Canada Ltd, 10 Alcorn Avenue, Toronto, Ontario, Canada M4V 3B2
Penguin Books (N.Z.) Ltd, 182-190 Wairau Road, Auckland 10, New Zealand

Penguin Books Ltd, Registered Offices: Harmondsworth, Middlesex, England

First published in the United States of America by Viking Penguin, Inc., 1987
Published in Picture Puffins, 1989

10   9   8   7   6   5

LIBRARY OF CONGRESS CATALOGING IN PUBLICATION DATA
Baum, Arline.
   Opt : an illusionary tale / by Arline and Joseph Baum.   p.   cm.
   Summary: A magical tale of optical illusions, in which objects
seem to shift color and size while images appear and disappear.
ISBN 0-14-050573-3
[1. Optical illusions–Fiction.] I. Baum, Joseph. II. Title.
[PZ7.B32670Op 1989]   [E]–dc19   88-28755   CIP   AC

Set in Plantin

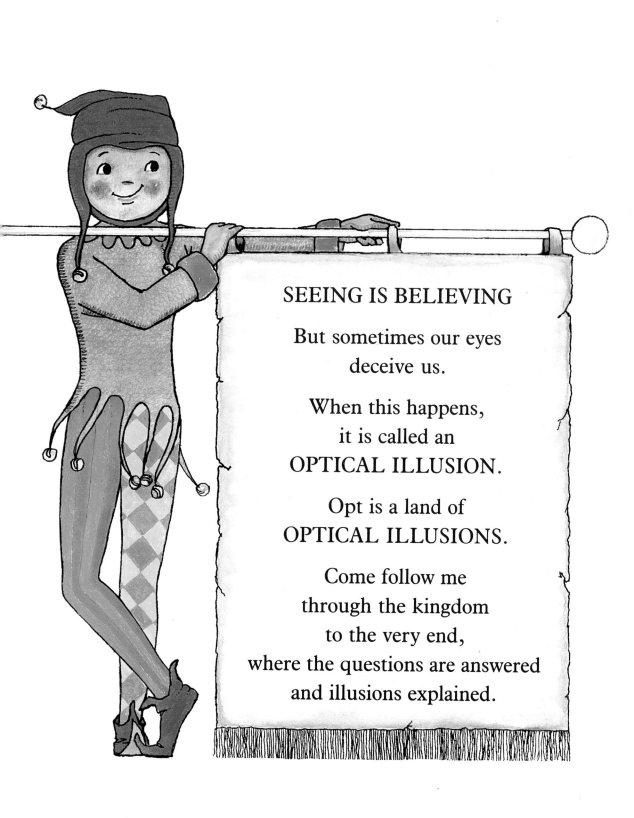

SEEING IS BELIEVING

But sometimes our eyes
deceive us.

When this happens,
it is called an
OPTICAL ILLUSION.

Opt is a land of
OPTICAL ILLUSIONS.

Come follow me
through the kingdom
to the very end,
where the questions are answered
and illusions explained.

A Sunny Day in Opt, a day of banners, balloons, and surprises

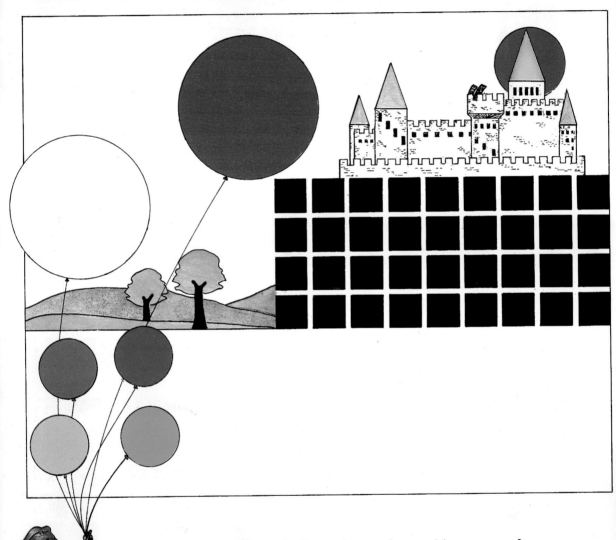

Can you make my balloon change from white to green?
For thirty seconds stare at the red. Now look at the white—is it green instead?

The Wall surrounding the castle

Where white lines cross, gray dots are seen.
One disappears where one has been.

The Castle Guard with his trident

How many prongs do you see?
I see two on the bottom—but on the top, three.

The Royal Messenger arriving with a letter for the King

The vertical lines of the messenger's cloak are crooked. The red tape on the letter is longer than the blue. But is this really true? Remember, now you are in OPT!

The Trumpeters announcing the arrival of the messenger

Who is smaller?

The King and Queen waiting for the message

Who is taller?

The Message for the King to read

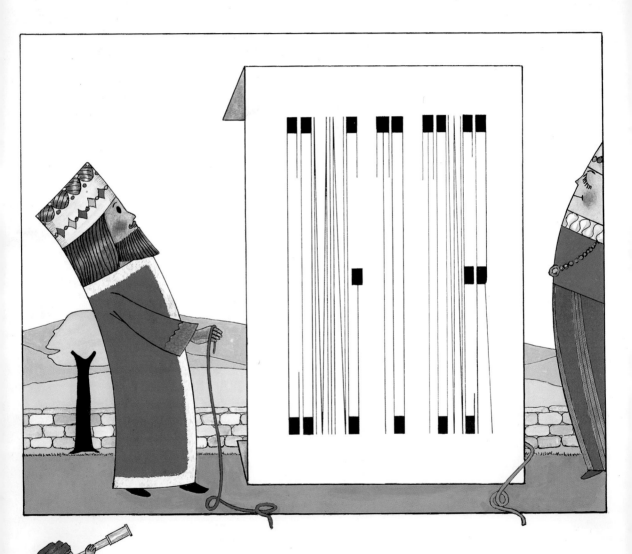

A clue to make the message clear.
First tilt the book, then take a look.
Who sent the message?

The Royal Art Gallery, dusted and tidied

Are the top of the lampshade and the top of the lamp base the same length?
Two ladies framed—or is it four?
Hidden elsewhere, you'll see two more.

The Prince goes fishing with his new rod

Which is the rod and which the branch of the tree?
Now look at the Prince's shirt.
What do you see?
Is the space between the shirt's black dots
larger than those same black spots?

The Princess picking a special bouquet

Flowers fair, flowers bright.
Which flower center is larger—the black or the white?

The Great Hall, ready for the party

Should the Queen straighten the mirror on the wall?
There are eight more faces. Can you find them all?

The Opt Sign pointing the way to the zoo

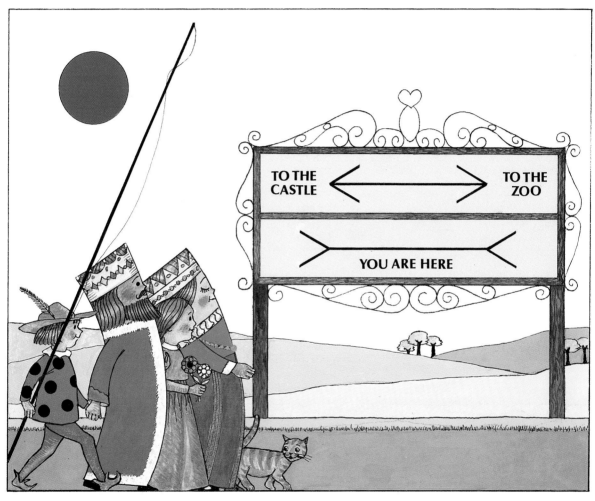

TO THE
CASTLE

TO THE
ZOO

YOU ARE HERE

By the sign the royal family will stop.
Which line is longer, the bottom or top?
The King knows who the guest will be.
So do I—just follow me.

The Opt Zoo, home of amazing animals

Faces within faces can be found—
if you just turn the book around.

The Zookeeper and the Royal Pet
hearing the news

Is the body of the royal pet shorter than its neck? Is the height of the zookeeper's hat the same as the width of its brim? For thirty seconds stare at the star that is blue. Now look at white paper—a colorful change, just for you.

The Pavilion decorated with banners

Are the banners light green or dark green, light pink or dark pink? Some say they're the same shade. But what do *you* think?

The Tower with guard spotting the guest

The guard marches up, stair by stair—but is he getting anywhere? He sees the guest. Who can it be? Turn the page and you will see!

The Guest is here!

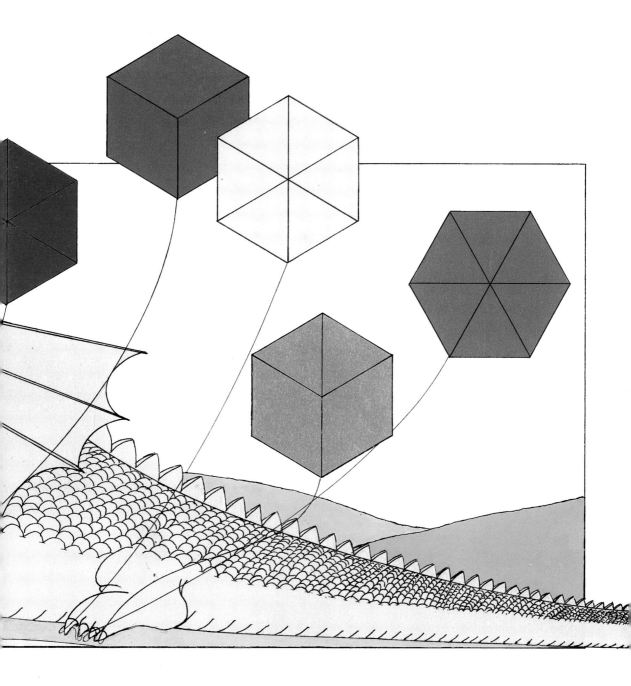

The fire-snorting dragon now comes in. Turn the book and his
eyes will spin. Arriving with presents—and none too late. But
did he tie the red ribbons on straight? Look closely at the
bright kites in the air. Do flat kites or box kites float up there?

The Birthday Party for the Prince

This gift, unwrapped, tells the Prince's age.
This is what the dragon said,
"Six blocks become seven if you stand on your head.
HAPPY BIRTHDAY!"

The Dragon saying good-bye

The dragon was a perfect guest. The party was a great success.
But *you* don't have to go away, come join me in Opt any day.

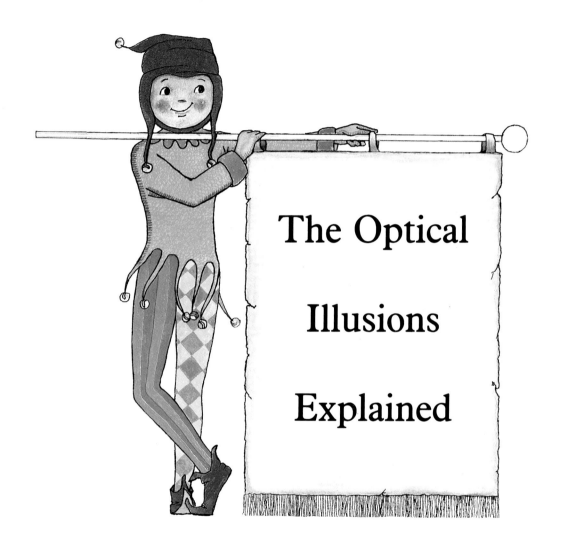

The Optical

Illusions

Explained

Some illusions have more than one explanation. Every day, scientists and researchers are learning more and more about why we see what we see. As more research and experiments are done, ideas change. We all see things differently, and this is what makes optical illusions so magical.

On the next five pages, you will find some answers and possible explanations for each scene, from sunrise in Opt to the Dragon's farewell.

A SUNNY DAY • *Page 4*

When you look steadily at the red balloon, part of your eye becomes tired. Then, when you look at the white balloon, a different part of your eye takes over. This part isn't tired, and it makes green, the complementary color of red, appear. This simplified color wheel shows complementary colors. They are the colors opposite one another on the wheel. (afterimage/eye-fatigue illusion)

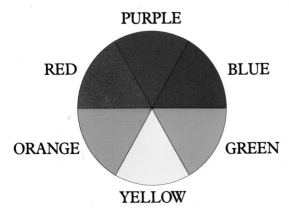

PURPLE

RED   BLUE

ORANGE   GREEN

YELLOW

THE WALL • *Page 5*

The white band is whitest when seen against the black squares. At the white intersections, however, there is no white-black contrast. If you look at these white squares out of the corner of your eye, they appear gray. If you look at the gray dots directly, they disappear. This is because your eye is weakest at its corner. (irradiation-contrast illusion)

THE CASTLE GUARD • *Page 6*

Cover the top of the trident and you see two prongs. Cover the bottom and the trident now has three prongs. You can draw this object, but you can't construct it. (impossible-object illusion)

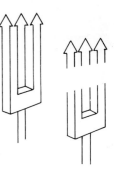

THE ROYAL MESSENGER • *Page 7*

Angles are sometimes tricky! The four white vertical lines on the messenger's green coat are parallel. The short lines drawn at an angle create the illusion.

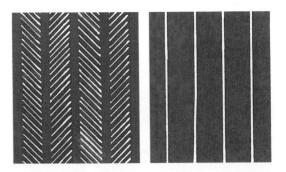

Hold the page a little below eye level. Tilt the book away from you, and the vertical lines become parallel. The angle of the tilt cancels out the illusion. (angle illusion)

The red and the blue tapes on the envelope are the same length. If you remove the outline of the envelope, you can see this. (geometrical-contrast illusion)

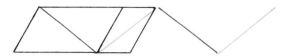

Have you seen any monkeys in the trees? Look for their profiles in the outlines of the treetops.

THE TRUMPETERS • Page 8

Remove the lines of the landscape, and you'll see that the trumpeters are the same size. Perspective is the key to this illusion. When objects move toward the horizon, they appear smaller. One trumpeter seems larger because he has not been drawn in proportion to the scene around him. (geometrical-contrast illusion)

THE KING AND QUEEN • Page 9

Reversing the position of the King or the Queen proves they are the same size. When line A is placed next to line B, the

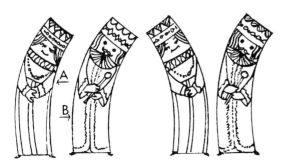

King appears larger than the Queen because we are comparing the two lines, rather than the whole figures. (geometrical-contrast illusion)

THE MESSAGE • Page 10

Hold the page a little below eye level. Tilt the book away from you, and the letters appear to shorten. If you close one eye, you can read the message: COMING TO TOWER. (word-perception illusion)

THE ROYAL ART GALLERY • Page 11

The top of the lamp-shade is the same length as the top of the lamp base. We're fooled again by putting a short length—the lamp top—next to a long length—the shade bottom. (geometrical-contrast illusion)

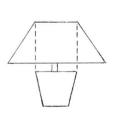

Here are two ladies, one smiling and one frowning. Here are two more ladies,

one young and the other old. The faces in the paintings seem to change. First you see one. Then, as your attention switches, you see the other. The brain cannot accept both pictures at the same time.

Look closely and you'll find two more faces on the sides of the table. (reversible-image illusions)

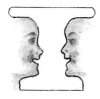

THE PRINCE • Page 12

The top line is the fishing rod. The bottom line is the branch. Were you fooled? When two parallel lines (the left and the right sides of the tree trunk) interrupt a line at an angle, it is difficult to follow the path of the line. (angle illusion)

The distance between the shirt's dots is the same as the diameter of the dots. Light areas appear larger when surrounded by darker areas. The purple, which is lighter than the black dots, makes the space between the dots appear larger. (irradiation illusion)

THE PRINCESS • Page 13

The black and the white centers are the same size. The white center appears smaller because larger circles surround it. The black center appears larger because smaller circles surround it. (geometrical-contrast illusion)

THE GREAT HALL • Page 14

The Queen does not have to move the mirror. It is perfectly straight. The angled lines of the curtain make the mirror appear crooked. (angle illusion)

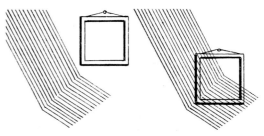

Did you find two faces on either side of the vase? And two faces on either side of the tables? Did you look closely at the candle?

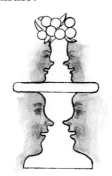

THE OPT SIGN • *Page 15*

Both lines are the same length. When the arrows point outward, the line appears shorter. When the arrows point inward, the line appears longer. (geometrical-contrast illusion)

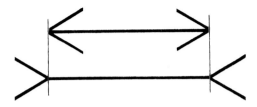

THE OPT ZOO • *Page 16*

Turn the book upside down and you will see different faces and animals. You recognize familiar details. You focus on the basic shapes of a letter or parts of a face and ignore the decoration around it. When you turn the book upside down, you focus attention on something different. The tail of the giraffe now appears as the head of a fish. Also, did you notice that the Opt Zoo sign reads the same, right side up or upside down? (upside-down illusion/word-perception illusion)

THE ZOOKEEPER AND THE ROYAL PET • *Page 17*

The pet's body is the same length as its neck, and the hat's brim and the hat's height are the same length. Vertical lines

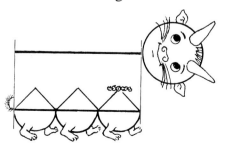

appear to be longer than horizontal lines. (geometrical-contrast illusion)

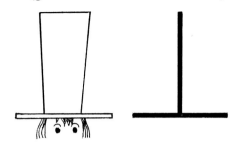

Did you follow the directions for the zookeeper's coat? This trick is similar to the balloon illusion on page 4.

THE PAVILION • *Page 18*

The shade of green on each banner is the same. The shade of pink on each banner is the same. The same color does not look the same when seen against different-colored backgrounds. (color-contrast illusion)

THE TOWER • *Page 19*

Follow the guard up all the stairs and you return to where he started without going down any stairs. It looks right, doesn't it? But the illusion is created by incorrect perspective. We would never really see a tower built like this. (impossible-object illusion)

THE GUEST • Page 20

As you stare at the dragon's eyes, your eyes become tired, because they have difficulty focusing on any one circle. This creates afterimages that make the dragon's eyes seem to shimmer.

To make the dragon's eyes seem to spin like wheels, rotate the book to the right or to the left. (afterimage/eye-fatigue illusion)

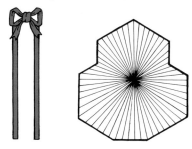

The ribbons are straight. Your eyes follow the lines that radiate out from the center of the gift. This makes the parallel lines of the ribbons appear curved. (angle illusion)

Sometimes the kites appear to be two-dimensional, made of six triangles, or a hexagon. Sometimes they appear to be three-dimensional box kites. It all depends on which lines you concentrate on. (reversible-image illusion)

THE BIRTHDAY PARTY • Page 22

You don't have to stand on your head! If you turn the book around, you should see seven blocks with white tops. The number of blocks you see depends on whether you view the boxes as having a white top or a white bottom. (reversible-image illusion)

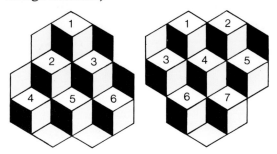

Look at the cat in her playtube. Will she come out from the right or from the left? Close one eye and she exits from the right. Close the other and she exits from the left. This is an illusion that can change direction at will because we can't see both exits at the same time. (reversible-image illusion)

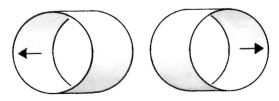

THE DRAGON • Page 24

We are so used to reading dark letters on a light background that it's hard to focus on light letters against a dark background. The dark spaces seem to be an abstract design instead of the words THE END. (word-perception illusion)

Making Your Own Illusions

If you trace the shapes of the King and Queen (page 9), cut them out, and put them side by side, you have an illusion that is deceiving. But if you draw and color characters on these shapes, you have put something of yourself into this illusion, something special. The shapes have become more than just shapes. They have become characters, and you have created them. Each is one of a kind! If you turn the shapes in a horizontal position, they can become caterpillars. What else can they be?

This can be applied to all the illusions. Imagination plays an important part in making your own optical illusions.

When doing *Color Illusions, don't forget to leave white space for testing.* Remember, you have to stare at the colored object for thirty seconds before you can see the illusion. Draw balloons, flowers, fancy costumes, using different-colored paper, crayons, or paint. Use some of the other illusions for patterns on the costumes (pages 7 and 17).

What happens when you color string-beans red, bananas or a pumpkin blue, grapes orange? Check the color wheel (page 25).

Remember, after you have followed the directions, the complementary colors will appear on your white paper.

Instead of looking at the white paper after staring at your picture, close your eyes. Do you see a smaller image of the same picture? You are *seeing* with your eyes closed!

Put red squares on white paper, as in the Castle Wall (page 5). Look at the white intersections for a few seconds, then look at a red square. Do you see a dark red cross on the red square? Try this with other colors.

The *Impossible Figures* (pages 6 and 19) are fun to trace. You can color the Tower, but try to color the Guard's trident. Impossible!

Make a garden of illusionary flowers (page 13). Use a compass or trace any round objects—different-size coins, for instance. Remember to make the centers of the flowers the same size. The petals can be different sizes. You do not have to

make flowers for this illusion. The figures can be Ferris wheels at a carnival, or bumper cars. What else can you think of?

The *Perspective Illusion* with the trumpeters (page 8) is another unbelievable illusion. Try this with dogs, cats, lions, or just about anything. Use three objects or figures instead of two. Make certain they are the same size and space them evenly in the landscape. You can trace the picture on page 8 to use as a background.

Reversible Images and Upside-Down Images are fun to do, too. Draw a profile of your friend, then make it the outline of a table or vase (pages 11 and 14). On pages 4 and 7 there are faces in the trees. Can you find other places to hide profiles?

Make an upside-down face (page 16). Here are two silly faces. A necktie becomes a feather, a bow tie becomes a bow in the hair, a mouth is a wrinkle. Do some funny animal faces. Fangs can flip into ears. Nostrils can become eyes.

When you look up at the clouds, do you sometimes see a dog or a bird or a bug that then dissolves into another form? Look at the trees. Do you sometimes see faces formed by the branches or the leaves of the tree? Your friend may see different faces and forms because each of us sees things differently.

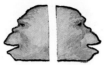

Many artists, such as Salvador Dalí, René Magritte, and M. C. Escher, found optical illusions fascinating, and painted pictures to fool and amuse the viewer. You can examine reproductions of their paintings in art books or perhaps see the originals in a museum.

So, you see, we live in a world of illusions. Illusions are all around us.